Kindergarten Countdown

Kindergarten Countdown

written by
ANNA JANE HAYS

illustrated by
LINDA DAVICK

Dragonfly Books ✈ New York

For Lucy,
with love
—A.J.H.

To my mom,
who sent me
to Miss Kay's
—L.D.

Text copyright © 2007
by Anna Jane Hays
Illustrations copyright © 2007
by Linda Davick
All rights reserved. Published in the
United States by Dragonfly Books, an imprint
of Random House Children's Books, a division
of Random House, Inc., New York.
Originally published in hardcover in the United States
by Alfred A. Knopf, an imprint of
Random House Children's Books, New York,
in 2007. Dragonfly Books with the colophon is
a registered trademark of Random House, Inc.
Visit us on the Web! randomhouse.com/Kids
Educators and librarians, for a variety of teaching tools,
visit us at RHTeachersLibrarians.com
Library of Congress Cataloging-in-Publication Data is available upon request.
ISBN 978-0-375-84252-8 (trade) — ISBN 978-0-375-94252-5 (lib.bdg.) —
ISBN 978-0-385-75371-5 (tr. pbk.)
MANUFACTURED IN CHINA
10 9 8 7 6 5 4 3
First Dragonfly Books Edition

My school starts in one week, so—
I have SEVEN DAYS to go.
Mom says be patient, do not worry.
But I can't wait! I'm in a hurry!

SCHOOL STARTS!

SOA
CUPCAKES
apples
COffee
cherries

7 days to Kindergarten.

I'll be ready, I'll be smart.
I will get a running start.
I'll say thank you,
I'll say please.
I will say
my ABCs!

Monday

6 days to Kindergarten.

I'll be ready,
I'll be good.
I will sit still
when I should.
I'll use a tissue
when I sneeze.
I will count
my 1-2-3's!

Tuesday

5 days to Kindergarten.

Yay!
Then I'll go to school
in flashy sneakers (oh so cool)!
I'll wear my superhero sweater
that makes me feel
strong and better.

Wednesday

4 days to Kindergarten.

I'm all set for show-and-tell
(and I can do it very well).
I'll bring my poKey little snail
and talK about his slimy trail.

Thursday

3 days to Kindergarten.

Three more days
and this weeK ends.
I can't wait
to maKe new friends!
We'll taKe turns
and play new games,
and practice writing
our own names.

2 days to Kindergarten.

Is it time to make my lunch?
Banana sandwich, ice cream crunch,
Popsicles, pickles, one lollipop.
At school I'll ask who wants to swap.

Saturday

1 day to Kindergarten.

Now it's time to pacK my stuff.
Hope my bacKpacK's big enough
for my picture booK and trucK
and shiny rocK to bring me lucK.

Sunday

School is just
one night away!

I brush my teeth and jump in bed
with letters and numbers in my head.
I will try to go to sleep
by counting Kindergarten sheep!

O days to Kindergarten.

I waited seven days to say—
Kindergarten starts today!

Monday

7 Monday

6 Tuesday

5 Wednesday

4 Thursday

3 Friday

2 Saturday

1 Sunday

0 Monday